21st Century Junior Library

Drills

By Josh Gregory

CHERRY LAKE PUBLISHING * ANN ARBOR, MICHIGAN

CHERRY
LAKE
Publishing

Published in the United States of America by Cherry Lake Publishing
Ann Arbor, Michigan
www.cherrylakepublishing.com

Content Adviser: Roger McGregor, Director, Hannibal Career and Technical Center, Hannibal, Missouri

Reading Adviser: Marla Conn, ReadAbility, Inc.

Photo Credits: Cover, ©INSADCO Photography/Alamy; page 4, ©Nagy-Bagoly Arpad/Shutterstock, Inc.; page 6, ©graja/Shutterstock, Inc.; page 8, ©Valerii Ivashchenko/Shutterstock, Inc.; page 10, ©sfam_photo/Shutterstock, Inc.; page 12, ©Dirk Ott/Shutterstock, Inc.; page 14, ©Marijus Auruskevicius/Shutterstock, Inc.; page 16, ©iStockphoto.com/dcdebs; page 18, ©Boobl/ Shutterstock, Inc.; page 20, ©donatas1205/Shutterstock, Inc.

LIBRARY OF CONGRESS CATALOGING-IN-PUBLICATION DATA
Gregory, Josh.
 Drills/by Josh Gregory.
     pages cm.—(Basic tools) (21st century junior library)
 Audience: K to grade 3.
 Includes bibliographical references and index.
 ISBN 978-1-62431-170-3 (library binding)—ISBN 978-1-62431-302-8 (paperback)—
ISBN 978-1-62431-236-6 (e-book)
 1. Electric drills—Juvenile literature. 2. Drilling and boring machinery—Juvenile literature. I. Title.
 TJ1263.G74 2013
 621.9'52—dc23   2013004926

*Cherry Lake Publishing would like to acknowledge the work of
The Partnership for 21st Century Skills.
Please visit www.p21.org for more information.*

Printed in the United States of America
Corporate Graphics Inc.
July 2013
CLFA11

CONTENTS

Drills make many home improvement projects faster and easier to do.

What Is a Drill?

Have your parents ever worked on a home improvement project? Maybe they built a wooden stool for the kitchen. Perhaps they attached a set of shelves to the wall. They probably used a drill for projects like these.

A power drill's bit spins as long as the trigger is held down.

Drills are tools that put holes in things. Most of today's drills are powered by electricity. They are called power drills. A worker simply presses a button. This makes the power drill's **motor** spin the **bit**.

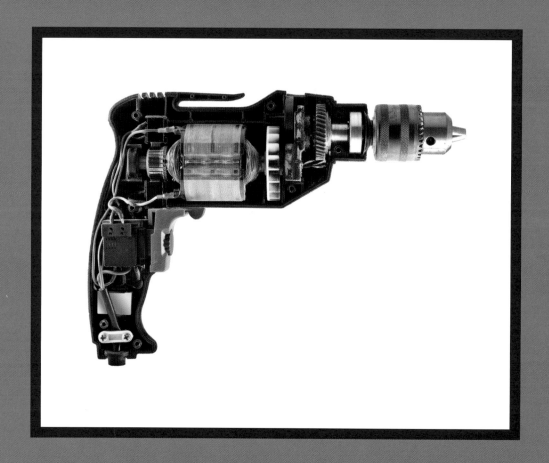

Most of a drill's inner parts are made of metal.
Metal is very durable, meaning it can last a long
time without breaking.

The motor and most other pieces inside the drill are metal. So is the bit. The outside of the drill is a hard plastic case. A drill also has wires inside. They move electricity from the power cord or **battery** to the motor.

Ask Questions! Do you know how electricity works? If not, ask your parents or teacher to explain it. You can also look for books to learn more about electricity.

Cut material moves up the bit's spirals and out of the hole. This keeps the hole clear and open.

How Are Drills Used?

Before using a drill, a worker first marks where to put a hole. The person then places the tip of the drill bit on the mark. He or she pulls a trigger. The drill bit spins. The bit's sharp tip cuts a hole into the surface. Spirals along the bit's sides move the cut material out of the hole.

Screws keep the parts of a bed frame and other pieces of furniture together.

Drills can be used to put holes in almost anything. Many people use them to make holes in wood. They can then put screws in the holes. This is useful for hanging heavy pictures on walls. It also helps attach two pieces of wood together.

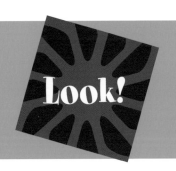

Look! Why might workers need to put holes in things? Look at some of the objects around your house. Do you see any that have holes drilled in them?

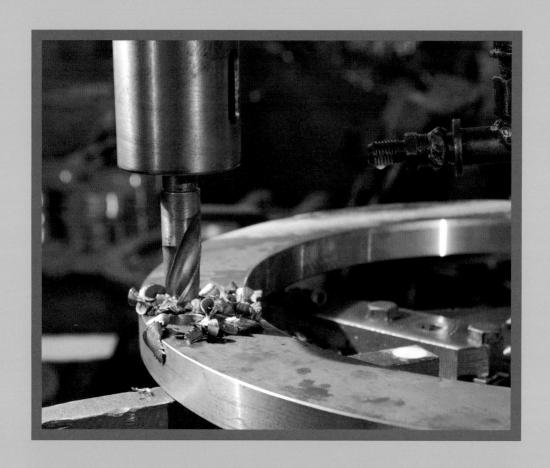

Drill bits have to be very tough to cut into metal.

Drills can also cut holes in plastic, metal, rock, and other materials. A worker might cut a hole in a piece of metal. Then it can be attached to another piece of metal with a **bolt**. Cutting into harder materials sometimes requires special drill bits.

Large drills such as this one are sometimes called
drill presses.

Different Kinds of Drills

Drills come in many different shapes. Most power drills have handles that curve down. Others are long and straight. These do not have curved handles.

Some drills are very large and heavy. They are not handheld. People use this powerful equipment to repair cars or build furniture.

Some people prefer to use hand drills for certain projects.

Before power drills were invented, people used hand drills to make holes. They held the drill in one hand. They turned a handle with the other hand. Turning the handle made the bit turn. Hand drills are still used today. But they are not as common as power drills.

Think!

What are some reasons to use a power drill instead of a hand drill? Can you think of reasons a hand drill might be used instead?

Grinders create sparks when used on some materials. As a result, workers often wear extra protection.

Power drills are not only used for making holes. Many drills allow users to change the bit. A user might attach a screwdriver bit or a **grinder** to the drill.

You've learned all about drills. Can you spot anyone using one of these tools? You never know what they might be building!

GLOSSARY

battery (BAT-uh-ree) a container that produces electricity

bit (BIT) the pointed attachment on a drill

bolt (BOHLT) a metal pin that screws into a nut to fasten things together

grinder (GRINE-dur) a rotating device used to wear something down

motor (MOH-tur) a machine that provides power to make something move

FIND OUT MORE

BOOK

Hanson, Anders. *Drills*. Edina, MN: ABDO, 2010.

WEB SITES

How It's Made—Drill Bits

www.youtube.com /watch?v=l1cv8Gfx5UM
Watch a video showing how drill bits are made.

How Power Drills Work

http://home.howstuffworks.com /power-drills.htm
Learn more about how power drills work and watch a video showing some uses for power drills.

INDEX

ABOUT THE AUTHOR

Josh Gregory writes and edits books for kids. He lives in Chicago, Illinois.